I0830775

SWAGGER WARS©

Confidence is the New Swag

Author - Joyce Lee

ISBN Hardback: 979-8-9930206-6-2

Library of Congress Control Number: 2025921054

Text copyright 2025 by Joyce Lee

Illustration copyright 2025 by Umair Ali

Visit us on the web - www.spirit-np.info

Dedicated to:

For the kids who rock taped-up sneakers
like they're limited editions.
For the ones who spit bars louder than the drip.
For every hallway underdog—
this one's for you. Stay swaggy.

I believe in you!

"The Real Flex"

They point at my shoes and laugh at the tape,
but swag isn't measured by logos or shape.
It's not in the labels, the price, or the brand,
it's how I keep walking when life makes demands.

They said I was out, they tried to decide,
but swagger's the truth that I carry inside.
It's not in the crown or the shine that you wear,
it's found in your courage, the way that you care.

Swagger's not money, not lights in a show,
it's standing up tall when the crowd tells you "no."
It's walking through whispers, refusing to fall,
it's speaking your name when they doubted at all.

Swagger's the spark that no label can buy,
it's the fire that grows when you're learning to try.
It's roots in the ground and a reach to the sky,
it's choosing your voice when the silence is sly.

So laugh at my sneakers, my hoodie, my phone,
I don't need your crown—I've built my own throne.
Swagger's not something you wear for a day,
it's the life that you live and the words that you say.

And when the last chant has faded away,
my swagger will stand, it will not decay.
Confidence lives where the truth won't disguise—
that's swagger, that's me, and it never dies.

-   **Joyce Lee**

CONTENTS

ROUND ONE:

CALLING OUT

CHAPTER ONE

THE HALLWAY ARENA

At Ridgeview High, the hallway wasn't just a place to get from one class to another. It was a scoreboard.

Every morning, the moment you stepped through the double doors, the judging started.

One glance at your sneakers could make you *in*. The wrong pair could put you *out*. A hoodie with the right logo? In. A plain one? Out.

Latest phone in your hand? In. Last year's model? Out.

There wasn't a handbook, but everyone knew the rules. The hallway decided everything. Who got noticed. Who got laughed at. Who walked tall and who kept their head down.

Jalen Carter knew the rules better than most. He felt them pressing on him every time he walked that stretch of lockers. His shoes were clean, but old—taped at the sole where they had split last spring. His hoodie was plain gray. His only accessory was a spiral notebook tucked under his arm. In the hallway's game, that made him background noise.

But Jalen didn't walk like he was begging to get in. Not anymore.

"Yo, Carter!"

The voice cracked like thunder. Jalen didn't need to look up to know who it was. Trevon Hale leaned against his locker a few feet ahead, flanked by Dre in his varsity jacket and Mace with his quiet eyes and heavy chain. Together, they weren't just a crew—they were *The Royalty.*

"Nice kicks," Trevon said, dragging his words slow, like he wanted them to sting. "Are those… Retro From-the-Trash? Exclusive drop?"

The hallway rippled with laughter. A couple of freshmen elbowed each other, waiting to see if Jalen would fold.

He glanced down at his sneakers. Old, sure. But scrubbed white last night. Taped at the edges because shoes didn't grow on trees. Still his. Still carrying him where he needed to go.

Jalen lifted his head. "Funny," he said, voice calm. "I didn't know they sold insecurity in your size."

"Ooooh!" The crowd reacted instantly. Lockers rattled as someone slapped one for emphasis. Even kids who barely knew his name stopped to watch.

Trevon's smirk wavered just a fraction, but he wasn't about to lose his stage. He let Dre laugh too loud and Mace stay silent, like always.

"You talk big," Trevon said, shifting his weight, "for somebody without receipts."

Jalen adjusted his grip on his notebook. His heart was thumping, but his face stayed steady. "Guess it's a good thing I don't need receipts to be real."

The air thickened. Then someone shouted from the other end of the hallway:

"Showcase flyer's up!"

Students surged toward the trophy case, buzzing like bees. A bright poster was taped in the middle:

RIDGEVIEW TALENT SHOWCASE – FRIDAY 7PM

Singers, Dancers, Poets, Bands.

Winner gets $250 + Social Media Feature.

Someone had already scribbled at the bottom in thick marker: *Confidence Is the Real Flex.*

Trevon's eyes flicked from the flyer back to Jalen. His grin came back sharp. "Perfect. Now we got a stage."

Jalen frowned. "For what?"

"For this," Trevon said, gesturing between them. "Me and you. Friday. Winner defines swag."

The hallway buzzed louder than before. Kids whispered, already picking sides. Dre clapped his hands together like the fight was booked. Mace stayed quiet, but his gaze lingered on Jalen like he was trying to read him.

Jalen could've walked away. Could've laughed it off. But then he caught his reflection in the trophy case—hoodie, taped sneakers, notebook in his arm. And he remembered his grandmother's words from the night before:

"You got it, J. You don't need to shine like them. Shine like you."

He swallowed once and said it out loud. "Friday."

The word dropped like a bass line, and the hallway reacted like a crowd at a concert.

Trevon grinned wider. "Bet."

The bell screamed overhead, sending students scattering. The crowd broke apart, but the buzz didn't die—it just spread. Trevon and his crew strolled off like kings returning to their castle.

Jalen exhaled, pulse still pounding. He didn't regret it. Not yet.

"Please tell me I didn't just hear you sign up for war."

Amaya appeared at his side, her backpack big enough to hide in, her afro puffs slightly lopsided from rushing. She was already grinning like she knew the answer.

"Not war," Jalen said. "A definition."

"Same thing," she shot back. "You ready for Trevon and his smoke machines?"

"Smoke fades," Jalen said, surprising himself with the confidence in his tone. "Real words don't."

Amaya studied him, then smiled. "Alright, poet. Guess it's Swagger Wars now."

They pushed through the tide of students, stopping at the bulletin board. Names were already scribbled on the sign-up sheet in different handwriting: dancers, singers, rappers. Trevon's crew had written **Royalty – Performance Set** in bold black letters that looked expensive.

The pen hovered in Amaya's hand before she shoved it at Jalen. "Sign it. Before your nerves talk you out of it."

Jalen's hand shook slightly, but he scrawled his name anyway: **Jalen Carter – Spoken Word.**

The ink looked small compared to Trevon's letters, but it was there. Real.

CHAPTER TWO

THE NOTEBOOK

Jalen's room wasn't much. A twin bed pushed against the wall. A dresser missing a handle. A poster of Allen Iverson taped up with the corners curling. The window rattled whenever the 97 bus groaned down the street, but he didn't mind. Noise was normal.

On his desk sat his spiral notebook. Notebooks, plural, really—stacks of old ones, some nearly falling apart from use. Tonight, the newest one sat open, pages filled with crossed-out lines and messy loops of ink.

Jalen leaned back in his chair, hoodie tugged over his head, pen tapping against the margin. Four days. That's all he had before the Showcase. Four days before he stood in front of the entire school with nothing but words.

He read a line he'd scribbled earlier: *Swag is the way I walk when the lights are off and I can't see who's watching.* He shook his head. Too clunky. He scratched it out.

"Boy, you gonna stab that paper to death."

His grandmother's voice floated in from the doorway. Jalen glanced up. She stood with her arms crossed, flour dusting the front of her shirt from the cornbread she was mixing. Her silver hair was pulled back, and her eyes carried that sharp warmth only grandmothers seemed to master.

"Just writing," Jalen mumbled.

"You always just writing." She stepped inside, glanced at the notebook, then at him. "That showcase got you pacing holes in the page?"

"Something like that."

She eased onto the edge of his bed with a sigh. "Tell me."

Jalen hesitated, chewing on his pen cap. "It's Trevon. Him and Royalty signed up. He called me out in front of everybody. Said the Showcase will prove who's really got swag."

His grandmother chuckled low, the sound like gravel rolling smooth. "Lord, these boys. Thinkin' swagger comes with a price tag."

"Everybody buys it, though," Jalen said, leaning forward. "The shoes, the chains, the phones—it's like the hallway's a runway. If you don't have it, you're nobody. And now I'm supposed to stand up there like I can compete with all that? What if I choke?"

His grandmother reached over and tapped the notebook. "What if you don't?"

Jalen stared at her. She had a way of flipping words back on him so they stuck.

"You think I always had nice things growing up?" she asked, raising an eyebrow. "We had one pair of Sunday shoes, and if they got scuffed, you polished them till your arm hurt. But you know what? Nobody could walk like me but me. That's swagger. Not what's on your feet, but how you use 'em."

Jalen smirked. "So you saying I should just walk funny?"

She smacked his arm playfully. "I'm saying you walk honest. You walk like you belong, even when they want you to believe you don't."

The words sank deeper than he wanted to admit. He closed his notebook slowly. "They're gonna laugh."

"Let 'em laugh," she said. "The question is, will they listen?"

Jalen exhaled. The thought of a whole gym watching him made his stomach twist, but something in her voice steadied him. He picked his pen back up.

Later that night, when the house settled quiet and the bus rumbled far away, Jalen sat at his desk again. The page glared back at him, waiting. He pressed the pen down.

They said I'm out because my shoes don't shine.
They said I'm out because my hoodie don't brag.
They said I'm out because I don't buy labels.
But labels don't define me.
I write my own tag.

He leaned back, reading the words aloud under his breath. Not perfect. Not polished. But it was real.

His phone buzzed. A text from Amaya: **Don't bail. I'll fight you if you do. Bring fire.** 🔥

Jalen chuckled, shaking his head. He typed back: **I'm writing. Happy?**

Nah. Be ready.

He closed the thread and stared at the lines again. The notebook was filling fast, but every new verse made him more nervous. Could his words really stack up against lights, music, and Royalty's flash?

He thought back to the hallway—Trevon's smirk, Dre's loud laugh, Mace's silent stare. They were playing to win, not just to perform.

Jalen scribbled another line.

Swag is my silence before the storm.
Swag is my voice when the mic is warm.

Swag is the echo they can't ignore,
even when my shoes ain't from the store.

He underlined it twice.

By midnight, his eyelids sagged, but his notebook was alive. He tossed it onto the desk and fell onto his bed, shoes still on.

The Showcase loomed in his mind, huge and impossible. But somewhere under the nerves, a spark glowed steady.

He wasn't Trevon. He wasn't Royalty. He wasn't labels.

He was Jalen Carter. And Friday, they were going to hear his name.

CHAPTER THREE

THE SIGN-UP

By Tuesday morning, the Showcase sign-up sheet looked like it had been through battle already—ink smudges, doodles in the margins, and at least one tear where someone had pressed too hard trying to claim a slot. The hallway around the bulletin board buzzed like a marketplace.

Amaya dragged Jalen by the sleeve. "You're stalling."

"I'm thinking," he said, clutching his notebook tighter.

"You're doubting," she corrected. "Big difference. Doubt is boring."

Jalen rolled his eyes, but his chest was tight. Kids crowded the board, pointing at names like they were betting on fighters.

"Royalty's already locked in," someone whispered.

"They're bringing a DJ. My cousin said they rented lights too."

"Yo, it's over. Carter don't stand a chance."

Jalen heard it all, each comment sticking to him like gum on the sole of his shoe. He swallowed. His pen was somewhere in his backpack, but his hand felt heavy at the thought of using it.

Amaya shoved him forward. "Do it."

Jalen stepped up to the board. Names stretched across the sheet in every style imaginable—bubble letters, graffiti tags, careful cursive. There it was: **Royalty – Performance Set.** Trevon had written it in bold black ink that looked almost expensive, letters carved like a signature on a throne.

Jalen uncapped his pen. His hand shook just enough that he had to steady it against the wall. He pressed the tip to the page.

Jalen Carter – Spoken Word.

The letters looked smaller than Trevon's, but they were there. Permanent.

Behind him, the whispers flared.

"No way. He's actually doing it."

"Spoken word? Against Royalty? He's cooked."

Amaya shoved her way to the front, grinning like she'd just won a bet. "Told you," she said loudly enough for half the hallway to hear. "It's official. Swagger Wars."

The phrase spread like wildfire. By the time the first bell rang, kids were already chanting it under their breath.

In English class, Jalen kept his head down, but he could feel eyes on him. Even Ms. Patel raised her brows when she called his name for attendance.

At lunch, things exploded.

Two tables had merged into one giant debate pit. Kids argued with mouths full of pizza, waving their hands like lawyers in court.

"Trevon's got this. No question."

"Man, Jalen got bars, though. You ever hear him in class? Dude's pen is sharp."

"Bars don't beat beats."

"Royalty's got production value. It's a whole show."

"Words hit harder than lights. You'll see."

Jalen sat at his usual table, pushing fries around, notebook resting open beside him. Every so often someone walked past, pointing. Some gave him nods of respect. Others smirked like he was doomed.

Amaya, halfway through her juice box, leaned across the table. "Look, they're already picking sides. You wanted to change the definition of swag? Well, congratulations—you just became the definition of drama."

He groaned. "That's not comforting."

"Wasn't meant to be," she said. "It's motivation."

By seventh period, the buzz reached the teachers. Ms. Sato, who ran the Showcase, stepped into homeroom with her clipboard. She scanned the class, eyes landing on Jalen.

"I see some of you signed up," she said, tone even but pointed. "That's good. That's brave. But understand something—this isn't just about winning. It's about showing up. You got a slot, you perform. No ghosting. No excuses."

Her eyes lingered on Jalen a beat longer before moving on. His ears burned.

Walking home, Jalen tried to drown the noise with music, earbuds blasting an instrumental beat. But the whispers clung to him.

"You're crazy for going against Trevon."

"Royalty's got the whole school hyped."

"Spoken word? That's not even swag."

He tightened his grip on his notebook. Every comment felt like a push, daring him to back out.

At the corner store, he stopped to grab a drink. A group of freshmen were inside, huddled around a rack of chips. One of them glanced up, eyes widening.

"Yo, that's him," the kid whispered.

Another nudged him. "That's Carter. Swagger Wars."

Jalen froze. He wasn't used to being noticed outside of school walls. The freshmen looked at him like he was already part of a story they'd be retelling. He gave them a small nod and left before they could ask more.

That night, Amaya blew up his phone.

Amaya: People are talking. You trending in the cafeteria.
Jalen: Not sure that's a good thing.
Amaya: It is. Royalty got lights. You got words. Let them clash.
Jalen: Whole school's expecting me to choke.
Amaya: Then don't.
Jalen: Easier said than done.
Amaya: Nah. Easier written than undone. Get back to that notebook.

He stared at her last message. Easier written than undone. He flipped open his notebook.

They want me silent, stuck on the edge.
They want me chasing brands like a pledge.
But swag ain't a price tag stitched on a sleeve.
It's the voice in my chest that I still believe.

He wrote until his pen ran dry.

Wednesday morning, the school felt different. Flyers for the Showcase multiplied overnight, plastered across lockers and bathroom stalls. Someone even started a countdown on the whiteboard in the cafeteria: **3 DAYS.**

The whispers had grown into factions. "Team Royalty" scrawled in marker on one side of the hallway wall, "Team Carter" on the other. Some kids wore paper crowns for Trevon; others carried notebooks as a nod to Jalen.

By third period, it didn't feel like just a talent show anymore. It felt like the school itself was split down the middle.

And in the center stood Jalen, caught between fear and fire, knowing he couldn't turn back.

ROUND TWO:

TAKING HITS

CHAPTER FOUR:

THE CREW DIVIDE

By Thursday morning, Ridgeview High felt like two schools stuffed into one building. The Showcase had split the hallways clean in half. One side crowned Trevon Hale and his crew *The Royalty* as guaranteed winners. The other half, quieter but growing, whispered that maybe, just maybe, Jalen Carter had something real enough to shake the throne.

It showed in the little things. The cafeteria split into two camps—one group blasting music from a Bluetooth speaker, shouting Royalty's catchphrases, while another gathered in a corner, notebooks out, scribbling lines like they were training for battle. The art kids even started sketching mock posters: *"Royalty Reigns"* in gold letters versus *"Carter's Words Cut Deeper"* in bold black.

Jalen hadn't asked for any of it, but there it was.

At his locker, Jalen pulled out his math book, trying to keep his head down. But a kid from his history class sidled up, grinning.

"You got this, Carter. Don't let Tre clown you."

Before Jalen could answer, another voice cut in. "Don't waste your breath. Royalty already won. They got lights, beats, the whole package. Dude's just gonna stand there with a notebook."

The two students glared at each other, arguing over him like he wasn't standing right there. Jalen shut his locker with a sharp click.

"Appreciate the support," he muttered, walking away before they dragged him deeper into it.

At lunch, things hit a boiling point.

Royalty held court at their usual table, the center of the cafeteria. Trevon leaned back with his arms spread like he owned the place. Dre was mid-story, hyping their rehearsal.

"Bro, we got choreography, lights, and a DJ. It's over. Carter won't even show."

"Don't bet on that," a voice called. Heads turned. Amaya stood on a chair at Jalen's table, notebook in hand. Her grin was daring. "Carter's not just showing. He's shutting you down."

The cafeteria roared. Some kids clapped, others booed.

Trevon raised an eyebrow. "That so?"

"Facts," Amaya shot back. "Royalty's rented swag. Jalen's got real swag."

The room buzzed with *ooooohs.*

Jalen buried his face in his hands. "Why'd you do that?" he groaned when Amaya sat back down.

"Because," she said simply, "if they're gonna talk, let's give them something worth saying."

The rest of the day, Jalen couldn't escape it.

In science, kids slipped him folded notes: *"Go get 'em."*
In gym, a group of juniors started a chant: *"Swagger Wars! Swagger Wars!"* until the coach barked at them to cut it.

In art class, someone sketched a cartoon of him facing Trevon like boxers in a ring.

By last period, Jalen's head throbbed. He shoved his notebook into his backpack and headed for the door. That's when Mace appeared, leaning against the lockers like he'd been waiting.

"You good?" Mace asked, voice calm, low.

Jalen hesitated. "What do you care?"

Mace shrugged. "I don't. Not like that. But… pressure's pressure. Just wondering if you're gonna fold."

Jalen bristled. "You think I will?"

Mace studied him, unreadable. "Don't know. Royalty? We got flash, yeah. But flash burns out. Sometimes real sticks harder. Depends if you bring it."

Before Jalen could reply, Mace pushed off the lockers and walked away, leaving his words behind like a challenge.

That night, Jalen sprawled across his bed, notebook open. He scrolled through social media—memes about *Swagger Wars* filled his feed. One had a picture of Trevon in a crown. Another showed a blurry shot of Jalen in the cafeteria with the caption: *"The Underdog Poet."*

He closed the app before it ate him alive.

Amaya's texts pinged again: **You see this? They already making memes. You're famous.**

Jalen: Not famous. Target.

Amaya: Target? Nah. Headliner. Don't mess it up.

He tossed the phone aside and stared at his notebook. His verses stared back, jagged and uneven. They didn't look like weapons. But maybe they could be.

Swag isn't bought in a store.
Swag is the courage to walk through the door.
Swag is the truth that they can't ignore.
And when I speak, they'll hear me roar.

He read it aloud, voice shaky at first, then stronger.

Outside his window, the bus roared past, headlights flicking across his wall. Inside, Jalen's own roar was still growing.

By Friday morning, Ridgeview wasn't just a school—it was a battlefield waiting for its showdown. And Jalen Carter was right at the center, whether he liked it or not.

CHAPTER FIVE:

PRACTICE MAKES PRESSURE

By Thursday evening the school felt like a drum you could hear from home. Even in Jalen's room, with the window shut and the heater ticking in the corner, the Showcase thumped in the back of his head—boom, boom, boom—counting down.

He cleared a path on the floor between his bed and the postered wall. The poster—Allen Iverson crossing someone into retirement—watched him like a coach. Jalen set his phone on the dresser, hit record on the camera, and stood in the center of his room with his spiral notebook.

"Okay," he told the empty air. "No shrinking."

He stared at his opening lines. His mouth felt dry. He closed the notebook, then opened it again, then set it down altogether.

"From the top," he said, and started.

"My swag isn't stitched in a sleeve

it's the breath I catch and the ground I leave—"

He stumbled. Too fast. He reset. Again.

"My swag isn't stitched in a sleeve—"

He heard his voice come out thin and pressed, like it was squeezing through a straw. He stopped the recording and watched the playback. There he was on the small screen:

hunched shoulders, eyes down too much, hands stiff at his sides like he was being searched.

He winced. "Nah."

He tried again with the notebook closed, forcing his eyes up.

"My swag isn't stitched in a sleeve,
it's the breath I catch and the ground I leave—
it's the 'no' I owe to the lies they preach,
it's the yes inside that I finally reach."

Better. Still tight. His hands didn't know where to live. He set the notebook on his bed and practiced with empty palms, letting them rise when the words rose, fall when the words fell. He tried stepping forward on the word *yes*. He tried a pause after *preach*. He played the video. This time, he didn't hate it. He didn't love it either.

His phone vibrated with three quick dings. Group chat: **Ridgeview Rants**—a hundred students and a thousand opinions. He shouldn't open it. He opened it.

vid: ROYALTY REHEARSAL 🔥🔥🔥

He tapped.

The gym was dark except for a wash of purple lights and a row of LED tubes strobing like lightning. Trevon walked through fog that rolled off the stage like a living thing. Dre hyped him from the side. The beat hit with a chest-thump. Trevon stepped into the center, grinning, then snapped into a move that made the room scream. Mace came in on the second eight-count, smooth and surgical. The camera shook from whoever was filming because they couldn't stay still.

The comments scrolled like rain:

Bro this is SUPER BOWL energy.
Carter finna read a poem next to THIS?
Crown him now.
Lights got lights.
Dang I might vote Royalty, ngl.

Jalen thumbed the volume down until the video played in silence. Without sound, the lights looked even louder. He felt his room shrink.

He turned the video off and set the phone face down. He stared at the floor. He could feel the cheap carpet under his socks. He could feel the heater humming and the faint rattle of the bus at the end of the block. He could feel his own heart pushing against his ribs like it wanted out.

He picked the phone back up, then put it down again.

He picked up the notebook instead.

"You're not them," he said to the paper. "So stop trying."

He crossed out a line he'd loved yesterday and wrote a new one.

If you came for a light show, close your eyes.
If you came for a truth, keep them open.

He traced the sentence, letting the words settle. He read the whole piece out loud in a whisper, found the clunky part, cut it in half. He moved a stanza to the top, then back down. He circled *labels don't decide me* and replaced it with *labels don't define my lines.* Cleaner. Less poster, more poem.

The door creaked. His grandmother peeked in, wiping her hands on a dish towel. "You want tea?"

"I want a new throat," he said.

"You'll work with the one God gave you," she said, stepping in. "Show me where you stand."

He cleared his throat and stood in the space he'd carved. She leaned on the doorframe, arms crossed, eyes soft but exact.

He started again, slower. He let the first line breathe. He stopped looking at the notebook and looked at her. She nodded once—keep going.

When he finished, she didn't clap. She stepped closer and fixed his hood, as if that would fix anything.

"You sound like you're trying to talk fast enough to outrun your nerves," she said.

"Because I am," he said.

"Hmm." She tilted her head. "Start again. This time, talk like the room is late and needs to catch up to you."

He blinked. "What does that even mean?"

"Own your pace, boy." She tapped his chest—once, twice. "They follow this, not the lights."

He tried again, slower, setting each word down like a brick. He looked at the corner of the room where the paint chipped and pretended it was the back row of the gym. He looked at the top of the poster and pretended it was the booth. He looked back at his grandmother and pretended she was every kid who had ever looked away because looking hurt.

When he finished, she smiled with one side of her mouth. "Better."

"Enough?" he asked.

"Better," she repeated, which meant *keep working*.

After she left, he texted Amaya: **Royalty got lights like it's a concert.**

Amaya: Good. Let them blind themselves. We'll listen.
Jalen: What if the crowd doesn't?
Amaya: Then we make them. Send me the new opener.

He sent the first four lines. The typing bubble appeared, disappeared, then came back.

Amaya: That second line slaps. The third is a little poster-y. Make it sound like you and not a wall sticker.

He laughed out loud. He cut the line and wrote a leaner one.

It's the yes I give myself, out loud.

He practiced until the heater cut off and the room felt cold again. He filmed two takes and watched them back. On the second, his hands looked like they belonged to him. On the second, there was a part where his voice cracked on *believe* and it didn't sound like weakness; it sounded like something opening.

He saved that take and labeled it **Maybe**.

His thumb hovered before he opened Instagram. The top story: **@Royalty_RVX**—a boomerang of Trevon flipping the mic and catching it, captioned **"Friday = Coronation 👑"**. The little crown emoji glowed like a dare.

He tapped on the next story: a poll.

Who's winning the Showcase?

◉ Royalty

◯ Carter

The Royalty circle was fat and smug at 78%. Carter was a thin line at 22. The numbers burned and he couldn't look away.

His phone lit again: **Amaya:** DO NOT LOOK AT POLLS.

Too late.

Amaya: We're not playing popularity. We're playing truth. Show up like truth.

He breathed in for four, out for six, like Coach taught him in freshman PE when he panicked before the mile. His shoulders dropped a notch. The percentages didn't matter Friday when it was one mic and two feet and a room that might decide to listen.

He set the phone face down for real and turned on the voice recorder instead. He did a full run-through standing, then another sitting, then one whispering to make sure the words carried even when the volume didn't. He marked his breaths with little slashes. He drew a box around the line he wanted to land like a punch. He repeated the last four bars until they felt inevitable.

Call me out, I won't crawl back in.
Call me out, I say where I've been—
Out's for price tags, in's for men.
I walk in with nothing—and leave with my skin.

He paused. Skin. Did that land right? He underlined *skin* and wrote **heart? name?** in the margin. He tried each out loud.

—leave with my name.
Cleaner. He circled it.

He stood in front of the mirror and tried on a half-smile that didn't apologize. He stood in front of the mirror and let his face be serious without being mean. He stood in front of the mirror and saw a kid who looked like a headliner in a gym with bad acoustics.

A new text blinked on the lock screen: a link from an unknown number.

u ready poet?

He frowned, opened the link, and it was another rehearsal clip—closer, slicker. This time Royalty had a backdrop with animated crowns. The beat dropped and confetti cannons fired in test mode, silver streamers floating down like money.

—Mace, another text followed.

Jalen stared. He typed: **Why send me this?**

The three dots thought for a long time.

Mace: Because Friday you need to know what you're walking into. Bring real. Don't try to match this. You can't. Don't need to.

Jalen's thumbs hovered. **Thanks**, he wrote finally.

Mace: Don't thank me. Win your way.

Jalen put the phone on the dresser and looked at his room again: the poster, the cracked paint, the notebook fat with edits. He could feel the beat from Royalty's video in his bones, but he turned it down in his head until all that was left was the click of the heater and his own breath.

He hit record one more time and started from nothing.

"My name is Jalen Carter.
I don't wear your crown.
I don't need your throne.
I brought my own ground."

His voice didn't shake.

He finished and let the silence after the last line sit for a whole count, then two. He didn't fill it. He trusted it.

When he checked the video, he didn't see a kid hiding behind a notebook. He saw a kid who'd chosen his pace and made the room catch up.

He saved the file and named it **Friday**.

Outside, a siren wailed and faded. Inside, the drum in his chest finally settled into a rhythm that felt like his.

Tomorrow would be hallway day—noise, chants, nonsense. He'd deal with it when it came.

Tonight, the practice had done what practice is supposed to do.

It turned doubt into work.

It turned work into voice.

And voice into something that might just carry.

CHAPTER SIX

HALLWAY BATTLES

Friday morning broke loud.

Before first bell, Ridgeview already buzzed like the inside of a speaker. Posters about the Showcase plastered the doors; someone had even stuck a paper crown on the school mascot. A whiteboard in the cafeteria read **TONIGHT: 0 DAYS** with a crooked smiley face under it. You could taste the hype, like metal on your tongue.

Jalen kept his hood down and his eyes level as he pushed through the flood. He'd slept okay—"Friday," the file on his phone whispered like a promise—but the school's volume tried hard to rattle him.

"Yo, Carter!" a freshman shouted, half-terrified, half-proud to know his name. "Spit something!"

Jalen lifted two fingers in a peace sign and kept walking. Not yet. Save it.

He turned the corner and nearly ran into a circle. The hall had opened up like a ring, bodies shoulder to shoulder. In the middle, two seniors were roasting each other's fits—freestyle fashion court.

"Why you got thunderbolt socks with business shoes?" one kid yelled. "You dressed like a storm that pays taxes."

The hallway howled. A teacher stepped in and tried to disperse them; they evaporated like mist and re-formed five feet down.

Royalty moved through the chaos like a parade. Trevon in the center, Dre flanking him with a portable speaker thumping a bassline, Mace trailing a step behind, eyes doing that quiet, collecting thing. Kids parted without thinking. More than once, someone shouted, "Coronation!" and the speaker kicked heavier.

Jalen felt it when they saw him.

"Good morning, Poetry Slam," Trevon grinned, stopping the procession. "Hydrated? Gonna need that voice tonight."

"Hydrated and unbothered," Jalen said. His tone landed calm, even though his heart had sped up. He kept the notebook closed at his side like a blade he didn't need to flash to use.

Dre cued the volume down and cupped a hand to his ear. "Hmm? Can't hear you over the sound of the LED budget."

Laughter sparked around them. Phones rose like a field of skinny mirrors.

"Funny thing about lights," Jalen said. "They don't change the words. They just make you see them."

"Oooooooh," the hallway chorused, hungry for a pre-show.

For a second, even Trevon's smile tilted. Then he clapped, exaggerated. "Bars. Cute. Tell you what—give the people a teaser. Thirty seconds. We'll give you a beat… you give us a bedtime story."

A chant bubbled up before Jalen could answer: "Teas-er! Teas-er!"

He cut his eyes to Amaya—already there somehow, sliding into his peripheral like a bodyguard. She shook her head once: *Don't give it away*. Save it. Make them wait.

"Tonight," Jalen said. "You get the full meal. I don't serve samples."

A bigger "oooooh." The kids who wanted blood booed, but not many. The pause made some of them lean in.

Trevon shrugged theatrically. "You heard the man—no samples. Must be rationing swagger." He lifted the mic-shaped water bottle in a toast and moved on, Royalty trailing in rhythm.

Jalen exhaled. He didn't realize he'd been holding the breath.

Amaya nudged him, proud. "You just won the pre-fight weigh-in."

"Feels like I just dodged a bus," he said.

"Same thing." She grinned. "Keep your feet under you."

They turned toward B hall—and walked into the first hit.

It started with a whisper that didn't want to be a whisper. Two sophomores on the lockers. "Carter," one said, too loud. "He really wearing those broke-boy fives?"

The other snorted. "Say it louder, maybe his shoes will hear the disrespect and peel off."

A giggle ripple.

Jalen's jaw tightened. He'd recorded "Friday" a dozen times last night. He'd slowed his pace and learned where the breath lived. He was not about to fight over shoes before homeroom. Still, the heat curled behind his eyes.

Amaya stepped forward as if she were answering attendance. "He's wearing clean shoes he cleaned himself. Revolutionary concept. Meanwhile, you skipped cleaning your jokes."

They blinked, as if no one had taught them what to do with pushback. Jalen didn't stop to watch the next lesson.

The second hit came ten minutes later, stealthy.

He was at his locker, grabbing his binder, when a scrap of paper floated down like a lazy snowflake and landed at his feet. He unfolded it.

A stick figure with a big head, tiny body. A crown on one side labeled **ROYALTY**. On the other, a crooked notebook with legs labeled **BORING**. Underneath, **Tonight: LULLABY L**.

He folded it again, clean and quiet, and slid it into his pocket. It could live there and become weight training.

Between second and third, the hallway turned arena for real. Someone—no one ever knows exactly who—started a clap pattern. Three slow claps. A breath. Three more. On the fourth, the chant rose:

"Tape. Those. Shoes." *clap clap clap*
"Tape. Those. Shoes." *clap clap clap*

It rolled like weather, gathering a wind. A few kids laughed and joined in—safe cruelty, the kind that hides in crowds.

"Tape. Those. Shoes."

Jalen froze mid-step. Heat hit the back of his neck. Something low and mean rose from his stomach and tried to stand up in his throat.

Amaya stepped hard into the noise. "Y'all practicing, or is this the performance? Because it's giving off-brand."

A few people snorted. The chant faltered, then doubled, louder—emboldened by itself.

"Tape. Those. Shoes."

Jalen's hands went numb, which made it easier to hold the notebook. He felt a current—there, the one the hallway always charged, looking for a body to light up. He almost turned. He almost ripped his hoodie off, almost threw the notebook, almost spit a verse wrong and ugly just to bleed the pressure.

A teacher's voice cut across the chant like a whistle through thunder. "Enough!"

Ms. Sato. She stood at the end of the hall, small frame, big authority. The clapping died, leaving a static hang. She walked straight to Jalen.

"You good?" she asked softly.

He nodded, not trusting the first sound his mouth might make.

She faced the hall. "We do not chant at people in this school. You want to chant? Chant for the teams on the court. You want to judge? Sit in the audience tonight and clap for the courage it takes to touch a microphone."

Silence. Somebody muttered, and she pinned them with a look that was somehow gentle and iron at the same time. "I said what I said."

She turned back to Jalen. "You owe them nothing before the stage," she said. "Walk."

He walked. Amaya walked with him, eyes throwing daggers in every direction like she had a supply.

Around the corner, away from the echo, Jalen stopped. He pressed the heel of his hand to his chest—one, two, three. His breath started to match his pulse again. He stood there a second, watching a tiny curl of paint peel from the cinderblock like a paper wave.

Amaya's voice softened. "You alright?"

"Almost wasn't," he admitted.

"That's legal," she said. "Almost doesn't count if you don't let it finish."

He huffed out a laugh. It shook. Then it settled.

By fourth period, the school had adjusted to its own embarrassment. The chant didn't return. A handful of kids who'd joined in earlier now pretended they hadn't. One slid a note onto Jalen's desk with no eye contact:

My bad. Do work tonight.

He didn't look back to see who it was. He just folded the paper and tucked it into the pocket with the cruel cartoon. Weight training. Balance.

In math, Ms. Chang caught his gaze while writing inequalities on the board. "Greater than," she said, marking the angle of the symbol with a flourish. "Remember—open mouth points to what's bigger."

He didn't know if she meant it for him. He took it anyway.

By last period, the temperature had shifted. Royalty still floated like a parade, but the current wasn't so simple. Jalen caught Mace watching him from across the hall, brows drawn. When their eyes met, Mace gave the smallest nod—a fraction, almost nothing— and kept moving.

On his way to the bus, Jalen stopped by the trophy case. Dust motes in the afternoon sun. His face in the glass: the hoodie, the shoes, the notebook. All the things they'd tried to make a punchline. He lifted the notebook and saw his reflection lift it, too. It looked less like a prop and more like a part of him.

He checked his phone. The poll had shifted to 68–32. Still lopsided. Less smug.

Amaya texted: **You ate that hallway. No crumbs. Meet me at six by the stage door. We do mic check together.**

Jalen: Ten-four, Coach.

He slid the cruel cartoon out again, then the apology note. He pressed them flat against each other, edge to edge, like two sides of the same coin. Then he folded both around the page with his final stanza and tucked the bundle deep into the notebook's back cover.

He stepped out into the evening. The air had that pre-game chill, the kind that made you breathe deeper. Cars idled in the pick-up loop. Somewhere down the block, a siren wailed and faded.

He imagined the gym six hours from now: the lights, the buzz, the first burst of applause when someone hit their mark. He imagined the silence he wanted after his last line—the kind that doesn't feel empty, only full.

He imagined the hallway tomorrow morning learning a new way to measure.

He didn't need the crown. He didn't need the throne.

He had his pace.

He had his ground.

He kept walking, and the door clicked behind him like a countdown.

CHAPTER SEVEN

THE QUIET ALLY

By late afternoon, the school emptied, but the buzz didn't leave with it. The Showcase owned the air now, thick enough to taste. Custodians wheeled carts down the hallways, prepping the gym for the night's showdown. Flyers fluttered from the walls like flags.

Jalen stayed after class, hunched over a desk in the back of the library. His notebook lay open, page scarred with arrows, cross-outs, and bold circles. He whispered lines under his breath, testing volume. The librarian gave him a look once but didn't shush him. Maybe even she knew tonight was bigger than homework.

He tapped his pen against the desk, trying to lock the rhythm into his bones. But nerves buzzed, chasing focus away. Every time he thought about stepping up in front of the whole school, the image of that hallway chant—*Tape. Those. Shoes.*—spooled back through his head.

He pressed his palms against the page. "Don't fold," he muttered.

A voice answered from the shadows of the next aisle. "You don't look like you're folding."

Jalen jumped, snapping the notebook shut. "Who's there?"

Mace stepped around the shelf, hands in his hoodie pocket, chain catching a sliver of light. He looked out of place among the dusty stacks, like a graffiti tag in a church.

"What you doing here?" Jalen asked, sharper than he meant.

Mace shrugged. "Looking for quiet. Found you instead."

Jalen eyed him, skeptical. "Trevon send you?"

"Nah." Mace slid into the seat across from him. His movements were slow, deliberate, like nothing could rush him. "Trevon don't know I'm here."

The words sat heavy.

"So why are you?" Jalen asked.

Mace leaned back, gaze steady. "Because I been watching. You don't move like the rest. That notebook's not just homework. That's… something else."

Jalen felt heat climb his neck. He wanted to deflect, crack a joke. Instead, he said, "It's all I got."

"Exactly," Mace said. "And that's what makes it dangerous."

Jalen frowned. "Dangerous?"

Mace tapped the table with one finger, slow. "Royalty's got flash. Lights, beats, smoke. That's what people expect. You? You're raw. Raw sticks. Flash fades."

Jalen blinked. He didn't expect that from one of Trevon's lieutenants. "So what—you rooting for me?"

Mace didn't smile, but his eyes softened. "I'm rooting for real. My sister writes. Poetry. She says words make your bones louder. When I see you, I hear bones."

The library hummed with its usual hum—air vents, a computer fan. Jalen stared at Mace, trying to read the angles. This was the guy who stood at Trevon's side, silent but sharp. Now he was here, handing him encouragement like a wrapped gift.

"You telling me this why?" Jalen asked finally.

Mace tilted his head. "Because I don't think Trevon understands what he's up against. He thinks this is just a show. You're not performing. You're testifying."

The word sat between them: *testifying*.

Jalen thought of his grandmother in church, eyes closed, singing like she was spilling something sacred. Maybe Mace was right. Maybe his poem wasn't just performance. Maybe it was testimony.

"I appreciate it," Jalen said carefully.

Mace nodded once. "Don't thank me. Just show up. Don't try to match us—you can't. That's the trap. Be you. That's the win."

They sat in silence for a moment, the kind that wasn't awkward but full. Then Mace stood. "See you tonight."

He walked away without looking back, disappearing between shelves like he'd never been there.

Amaya found Jalen ten minutes later, notebook back open, pen scratching fast. "Why you look like you just had an epiphany?" she asked, dropping her bag with a thud.

"Mace came through," Jalen said.

Her eyebrows shot up. "*Royalty* Mace? The chain guy? What'd he want—steal your metaphors?"

"No. He…" Jalen paused, still processing. "He told me not to try to match them. Said raw sticks harder than flash."

Amaya tilted her head, suspicious but intrigued. "Huh. Maybe he's not a mannequin after all."

"He said his sister writes," Jalen added, almost to himself. "That poems make your bones louder."

Amaya's face softened. "That's actually beautiful."

"Yeah," Jalen admitted. He looked at his notebook. "And true."

That night, Jalen sat on his bed with the house quiet, his grandmother already asleep. He flipped back through the pages of his notebook, searching for the heartbeat. He found it in the stanza he'd written two days ago, the one he almost cut:

They think labels decide the game.
They don't see me writing my own playbook.

He underlined it twice.

His phone buzzed. A text from Amaya: **Tomorrow we eat. Don't forget: no samples, whole meal.**

Another from an unknown number. **Bring real. Leave the rest. –M**

Jalen set the phone down and stared at the ceiling. For the first time all week, the weight on his chest felt lighter. He wasn't walking into this alone.

He had Amaya, he had his grandmother's voice in his ear, and now—even in a strange, quiet way—he had Mace.

And most of all, he had his words.

He whispered them once before closing his eyes.

Swagger isn't a label. Swagger isn't a crown.
Swagger is standing when the world wants you down.

Sleep took him. Tomorrow, the Showcase would test everything. But tonight, for the first time, he believed he could pass.

ROUND THREE:

OWNING THE STAGE

CHAPTER EIGHT

THE LEAK

Friday morning started with tension in the air, sharp enough to taste.

The Showcase posters had doubled overnight, plastered across every hallway. Some gleamed with "ROYALTY REIGNS" in metallic ink, while others had been scrawled over with bold Sharpie messages like **"Confidence Is the Real Flex."** The cafeteria countdown now read **0 DAYS.**

Jalen moved through the halls with his hood down, notebook clutched against his chest. He felt every glance, every whisper. The chants from earlier in the week still echoed somewhere deep inside him, even if no one was saying them out loud today.

By lunch, the trap was sprung.

The lights dimmed over the main hallway, and a projector flickered to life on the far wall. Someone had rolled down the assembly screen. A heavy bassline rolled out, Royalty's logo stamped across the opening frame.

Then came the video.

Grainy footage of Jalen in his bedroom, practicing in front of his dresser. It was the take he'd saved but never shared—the "maybe" attempt, the one where his voice shook.

Onscreen, his words came out high-pitched, edited with chipmunk squeaks. Cartoon sparkles trailed his hands as he gestured. A canned laugh track rolled over his pauses. Finally, the screen froze on his face mid-blink, with a sticker crown boinging onto his head.

The hallway detonated with laughter.

"Yo! Carter bedtime story vibes!" Dre shouted from the corner, clutching the speaker remote like a prize.

Trevon leaned against the lockers, arms crossed, grin wide. He didn't need to say anything—the room performed for him.

Phones whipped up. The chant started fresh, cruel and loud:

"Po-et-TRY! Po-et-TRY!"

Jalen's stomach dropped through the floor. Heat rushed to his face. He gripped his notebook harder, fingers trembling. Every instinct screamed *leave.* Walk out, disappear, save what little you've got left.

But Amaya was already there, fire in her eyes. "You thieves!" she shouted. "That's not comedy—that's desperation!"

No one listened. The chant kept rolling.

Then, above the noise, a teacher's voice sliced through:

"Enough!"

It was Ms. Sato. She stood with arms folded, gaze like iron. "This is a school, not a circus. Clear the hall. Now."

The projector snapped off. Lights buzzed back to life.

Jalen didn't move. His breath came shallow, his chest tight. The cartoon image still burned in his mind.

Mace appeared at his side, hands buried in his hoodie pocket. "That wasn't me," he said, low.

Jalen stared at him. "But it was Royalty."

"I told Trevon it was corny," Mace said. His eyes didn't waver. "Doesn't matter what they put on a screen. You still got the stage. Question is—are you walking or folding?"

Jalen swallowed hard. He wanted to say *folding*. But when he pictured his grandmother waiting at home, expecting to hear how it went, the word stuck in his throat.

"I can't tell her I ran," he whispered.

Mace nodded once. "Then make tonight the only version that counts."

The day dragged. Classes blurred. Teachers talked, but Jalen heard only echoes of the projector's cruel edits. Still, somewhere underneath, Amaya's words pressed: *Whole meal. No samples.*

By the final bell, the gym was already being transformed. Stage lights hummed. Folding chairs lined the floor. The air buzzed with anticipation.

Backstage, performers tuned guitars, stretched, whispered prayers. Royalty dominated their corner with cables, cases, and confidence. Trevon spun a mic in his hand, a king waiting for coronation.

Amaya tugged Jalen's hood, then adjusted his shoulders. "Say your name first," she said. "Claim your ground. Then map it for them."

Jalen nodded, notebook pressed against his chest like armor.

The Showcase kicked off. A dance trio nailed a risky lift. A soprano held a note that shook the rafters. A comedian cracked jokes that landed better than expected.

The crowd roared for each. But the roar had a rhythm—loudest for Royalty.

Finally, Ms. Sato stepped to the mic.

"Next up—Royalty."

The gym thundered. Fog poured, beats slammed, crowns lit up in neon. Trevon prowled the stage like he owned it. Dre hyped. Mace moved sharp, precise. At the finale, confetti cannons blasted silver rain across the crowd.

The gym was a snow globe of noise.

When the smoke cleared, Ms. Sato scanned her clipboard. Her voice steadied the air. "And now… Jalen Carter. Spoken word."

The spotlight shifted. Phones lifted. The gym hushed.

Amaya squeezed Jalen's hand. "Whole meal," she whispered.

He rose, notebook in hand, and walked toward the curtain.

His sneakers squeaked once on the hardwood.

The spotlight warmed his face.

And then—

CHAPTER NINE

FIRE IN HIS VOICE

The silence was heavier than noise.

Jalen stood in it, notebook on the stool, mic in hand. His palms slicked, but his chest held steady.

He breathed once, twice. Then—

"My name is Jalen Carter."

The sound cracked, but he let it stand. The gym leaned closer.

He began.

Jalen's Poem – Confidence Is the New Swag

My name is Jalen Carter.
I don't wear your crown.
I don't need your throne.
I brought my own ground.

You say I'm out 'cause my sneakers are taped,
but swag ain't leather, it's how you escape.
You say I'm out 'cause my hoodie's too plain,
but swag is the fire that burns in my name.

Swagger's not cash stuffed thick in your jeans,
not fog machines or crown emojis on screens.

Swagger's not chains that clink when you flex,
swagger is the courage to face what comes next.

It's not in the beats that shake the gym floor,
it's in the silence that waits when you open the door.
Not the lights that flash, not the gold that shines,
swagger's the backbone stitched into my spine.

I walk these halls with shoes you clown,
but every step still shakes the ground.
I wear this hoodie—gray, no tag—
but every word I speak is swag.

Swagger is breath when the chant gets cruel.
Swagger is standing when the hallway's the tool.
Swagger is saying my name out loud,
swagger is walking alone through a crowd.

So mock my sneakers, go count your chains,
I'll count my scars, my lessons, my gains.
Swagger's not bought in the mall down the street,
swagger's what grows when you refuse defeat.

Swagger is raw, unbent, unbroke.
Swagger is truth that refuses to choke.
Swagger is bones louder than noise,
swagger's in girls and swagger's in boys.

It's the notebook I carry, the lines that I write,
the voice I found in the middle of night.
Swagger's the yes when the world says no,
swagger's the seed that still dares to grow.

So when you ask who owns this stage,
I won't point to crowns or the brand-new rage.
Swagger is me—uncut, unmasked.
Swagger is confidence, built to last.

So hear me now, don't miss the call:
swagger is not in your closet at all.
Swagger's the truth that lives bone-deep.
Swagger's the vow I promised to keep.

Swagger is me—raw, unbent, free.
And that's the flex you'll never take from me.

The last line dropped like a weight.

For three seconds, no one moved.

Then—one clap. Two. Then the wave crashed.

The gym exploded. Bleachers shook. Students pounded rails. Teachers stood. Even Royalty's corner couldn't drown it out.

From backstage, Amaya screamed, "LOUD BONES!"

Jalen lowered the mic. His hands trembled, but he didn't hide them. He bowed once, calm, steady. Then he picked up his notebook and walked offstage.

The roar followed him.

Backstage, chaos swirled. Performers buzzed. Crew shouted cues. Ms. Sato hustled with her clipboard.

Amaya threw her arms around him. "Bruh, you didn't just perform—you set the place on fire."

Jalen laughed shakily. "I didn't choke?"

"You made *them* choke on their own noise," she shot back.

Ms. Sato appeared briefly, eyes soft. "You shifted the air in that room. Hold onto that." Then she was gone.

Jalen leaned against the wall, chest still humming. He pictured his grandmother's smile, how she'd glow when she heard.

Then he saw Royalty.

Trevon sat forward, smirk dimmed. Dre scrolled furiously, muttering. Mace, though—Mace watched Jalen, and for the first time, smiled.

Not mockery. Not pity. Respect.

Jalen nodded. Mace nodded back.

No words. No need.

Intermission broke. Lights rose. The crowd spilled into hallways, buzzing with quotes:

"Swag ain't leather, it's how you escape."
"Swagger's the backbone stitched into my spine."
"Swagger's what grows when you refuse defeat."

Jalen sat with his notebook on his lap, steady now. Amaya beside him, grinning.

"See?" she said. "No fog machine can drown truth."

And for the first time in a long time, Jalen believed her.

They had heard him.

That was enough.

CHAPTER TEN

SWAGGER WARS

Intermission tasted like electricity.

The gym lights came up just enough for people to breathe, and the crowd spilled into the hallways in a flood—buzzing, arguing, replaying lines like clips. The confetti from Royalty still clung to shoes, but Jalen's words clung to people's faces. You could see it: a look like they'd swallowed something true and were still deciding what to do with the flavor.

Backstage, Jalen sat with his back against a cinderblock wall, the cool seeping through his hoodie. His notebook lay across his knees like a landed bird. Amaya paced in front of him, grinning at strangers and daring any bad energy to try her.

"You hear them out there?" she said, jerking her thumb toward the gym. "That's not hype. That's hearts reloading."

He tried to laugh and only managed half a smile. "I felt… steady. That was new."

"Steady is a superpower," she said. "You went Captain Mic."

Ms. Sato popped her head through the curtain, cheeks flushed from corralling performers. "Excellent set. Stay close for the finale; we'll announce results after the last act." She paused, softer. "Whatever the scoreboard says, you already did the thing that matters."

He nodded. He believed her more than he thought he would.

Royalty settled on a row of folding chairs, unusually quiet. Dre scrolled with fast, agitated thumbs. Mace leaned forward, elbows on knees, looking like someone who'd been planning to say nothing and found himself wanting to say something anyway. Trevon rolled a mic in his palm, not spinning it this time—just holding it like it was heavier than he'd expected.

He stood and walked toward Jalen. Amaya's eyes sharpened; she stepped half in front without making it obvious. Trevon clocked the move and stopped two feet away, hands up like he came in peace.

"Good set," he said. Not grinning. Not sneering. Just the words.

"Thanks," Jalen said. His voice didn't wobble.

Trevon studied him for a beat. "You know if we win, they're gonna say it's 'cause of the lights."

"And if I win, they'll say pity points," Jalen said.

"People always got a reason." Trevon's gaze flicked to the curtain, where the crowd murmured like weather. "But you did your thing."

"So did you," Jalen said. Not a lie. Royalty's show had been a machine.

Trevon's jaw ticked; something like respect flashed and hid. He nodded once, then turned away, the conversation ending where it needed to.

Mace stayed. "Whatever they say," he told Jalen quietly, "tonight can't unsay what you said."

Jalen accepted the sentence like an amulet and tucked it into his chest pocket.

The second half of the Showcase rolled on: a drummer who played with sticks that glowed, a comedy duo whose jokes mostly landed, a soprano who sang like the gym had cathedral ceilings. Jalen clapped for all of them, really clapped—palms stinging. The stage felt less like a battlefield now and more like a place where people brought what they had and set it on the table.

Then the last act bowed, and Ms. Sato returned to the center, holding a clipboard like a verdict.

"Thank you, Ridgeview!" she called. The cheers washed in a wave. "You've been an incredible audience. Our judges have conferred, and… look, I'm not going to make a speech. I will say this: courage showed up tonight. All over this stage."

She glanced toward the side curtains—toward Jalen, he realized—and then down at her list.

"In third place, for that mind-bending footwork and fearless grin: **Lila Gomez**!" The gym whooped. Lila bounded up, flushed and delighted.

"In second place," Ms. Sato continued, drawing the moment just enough, "for a polished, high-voltage production that would make even a stadium blush: **Royalty**!"

The gym roared. A slice of the room stood before the rest, chanting, crown emojis practically hovering above their heads. Dre sprang up and whooped. Trevon's smile clicked back into place, a notch dimmer but still there. Mace clapped, nodding once to Jalen without looking at him.

"And in first place…" Ms. Sato said, and the gym leaned forward collectively, "for words that changed the air in this room: **Jalen Carter**."

The first scream that broke came from Amaya, shrill and triumphant. Then the bleachers erupted—kids pounding the rails, teachers whistling, parents standing with eyebrows raised like *well I'll be*, and a handful of Royalty fans clapping in spite of themselves because the moment simply pulled their hands apart and brought them together.

Jalen stood and couldn't feel his legs for a second. He walked anyway.

The light hit him warm and clean. Ms. Sato didn't hand him a crown. She handed him a plain plaque—wood, engraved plate, school logo. It looked like what it was: a marker, not a miracle.

She leaned in as he took it. "They heard you," she said. "Make it count."

He turned to the crowd. For a heartbeat, he met his grandmother's eyes in the top row. She had her hand over her mouth. When she moved it, he saw her smiling like a sunrise that knew every morning wasn't guaranteed.

He lifted the plaque once, not like a trophy, more like a signal. The noise swelled again. He didn't make a speech. He didn't need to.

Backstage, Royalty's corner was all edges and half-jokes. Dre shrugged theatrically. "Second is the first loser," he said, trying to laugh it off and missing.

"Second means next time, build a bigger show," someone said.

"Or a truer one," Mace said, almost under his breath. Dre didn't catch it. Trevon did. He looked at Mace, then at Jalen, then at the floor, recalculating a map only he could see.

He approached Jalen again, plaque still warm in Jalen's hands. For a breath, the noise outside became a dim ocean in another room.

"No hate," Trevon said.

"No hate," Jalen echoed.

Trevon held out a fist. Jalen bumped it. That was all. It didn't rewrite the past, didn't promise the future. It acknowledged the present: two kids who brought what they had and let a room decide.

Amaya slid in as Trevon moved off, eyes shining. "We did it," she whispered, like she'd been running uphill all week and finally reached a flat stretch.

"We did," Jalen said, and felt how true the *we* was.

They found his grandmother in the bleachers. She hugged him long and tight, murmuring things to his shoulder he'd want to remember forever: "Proud of you. You walked in like you belonged. You made them listen."

He didn't cry. He wanted to. He saved it for later, for a quiet place where the tears wouldn't be about the plaque at all, but about a hallway that tried to write his name and found out he had his own pen.

Monday tried to pretend it was just a Monday. The clocks ticked the same. The janitors rolled the same carts. But the hallway's scoreboard had been reprogrammed.

Someone had taped a new sign above the bulletin board, hand-lettered in thick black marker:

SWAGGER = CONFIDENCE.
(not labels)

Underneath, smaller: **Confidence Doesn't Come in Labels.**

No one admitted to writing it, but four different people took credit in whispers, which is how you know it belonged to everyone.

"Carter!" a freshman called as Jalen passed. "Bars!"

"Good work, kid," a teacher said, which at Ridgeview was like getting knighted and scolded simultaneously.

A little group had gathered near the trophy case, where Lila's third-place ribbon hung next to the Showcase poster. Someone had stuck Jalen's photo—a screenshot from the school's livestream—next to it. He looked serious and unlocked, mouth mid-line, eyes on a point beyond the camera. Whoever had printed it wrote a caption in ballpoint:
Own your ground.

Jalen stopped at his locker. There, taped to the door, was the cruel cartoon from Friday—**BORING** notebook vs. **ROYALTY** crown—only someone had drawn a big X through the bottom and added a third figure: a notebook with a megaphone, shouting lines that turned into lightning. Under it: **LOUD BONES.**

He laughed, surprise and gratitude swelling so fast he had to look at the floor.

Trevon's crew passed like always. The crowd parted out of habit, but something about the space was different now—less prostration, more courtesy. Trevon lifted his chin at Jalen, a gesture halfway between salute and see-you. Dre tried a joke about the plaque being made of particle board and nobody laughed. Mace peeled off as they moved on, just long enough to say, "Told you."

"Yeah," Jalen said. "You did."

"Keep the notebook on you," Mace said. "In case the hallway forgets."

"It will," Jalen said. "I won't."

Amaya hit him with a shoulder bump that almost knocked the plaque from his bag. "So," she said, "you gonna start the club?"

"What club?"

"Spoken word," she said, as if it were obvious. "Or call it *Confidence Club* if that's how we get funding. We put out prompts, run open mics, teach ninth graders how to spit their names like they own 'em. We make this permanent. We make loud bones the brand."

Jalen pictured it. A flyer on this same board. A circle of kids in a classroom after school, reading lines that sounded like the doors they'd been trying to open by themselves. A hallway that learned a different chant.

"Yeah," he said. "Let's do it."

They went to Ms. Sato at lunch, caught her mid-bite of a sandwich the size of a text-book. She listened, chewed, then nodded. "You write the proposal," she said to Jalen. "You design the flyer," she said to Amaya. "And you both host the first one next Thursday." She swallowed, smiling. "We'll call it… *Swagger Night*."

"Corny," Amaya said.

"Correct," Jalen said. "Perfect."

That afternoon, Jalen sat at his desk at home, the plaque leaning against the wall where the paint chipped. He opened the notebook he'd used all week and turned to a clean page.

At the top, he wrote:

Swagger Wars – Notes for the next thing

Underneath, without overthinking, he wrote:

If you came for the label, the tag will disappoint you.
If you came for the person, pull up a chair.

He stared at the words. He didn't cross them out. He didn't underline them either. He just let them sit, like the kind of sentence that might grow into a room.

From the kitchen, his grandmother called, "Dinner!" He closed the notebook and stood.

On his way out, he caught his reflection in the dark window: hoodie, old shoes, a kid who looked exactly like himself.

The hallway could keep its scoreboard. He had a different measure now—one that didn't need lights to work.

When he stepped into the kitchen, he said his name out loud because it felt good in his mouth.

"Jalen," his grandmother said, handing him a plate. "That's right."

Outside, the bus rumbled by, steady as a heartbeat.

Inside, he didn't need a crown. He didn't need a throne.

He had his pace.

He had his ground.

And that—finally, obviously—was the real swag.

"Jalen," his grandmother said, handing him a plate. "That's right."

AFTER THE WARS

Two weeks after the Showcase, the crown graffiti faded from the lockers. The confetti finally disappeared from the gym floor. But the words—the words didn't go anywhere.

They lived in the hallways now. In small ways first. A sticky note taped inside a locker: *Swagger is me.* A doodle on a math notebook: *Loud Bones.* A teacher quoting Jalen mid-lesson without meaning to: "Walk in with nothing, leave with your name."

By the end of the month, kids stopped saying *Swagger Wars* like it was a joke and started saying it like it was a reference point. Like an era.

The club idea Amaya had thrown out half-jokingly? It bloomed. Thursday afternoons, Room 214 turned into an open circle. A handful of freshmen read shaky lines at first, voices thin as paper. Jalen nodded through every word, then spit one of his own so they'd see it was safe. By the third week, desks filled the corners, and the floor was crowded with kids who wanted to try.

They called it *Swagger Circle.* Not polished, not official, but real.

Mace came once. He didn't read, didn't clap loud, but he sat in the back with his hood up and his chain tucked. Afterward, he pulled Jalen aside. "Not bad," he said. Which was Mace's way of saying everything.

Even Trevon drifted in one afternoon. No lights, no fog, no DJ. Just Trevon leaning against the wall while a sophomore girl read about losing her father and finding her voice in the same year. He didn't interrupt. He didn't laugh. When she finished, he clapped once, quietly, and slipped out.

Jalen's grandmother taped the Showcase program on the fridge like it was a diploma. Sometimes, when he walked past, she'd tap it and say, "Still proud." Sometimes she didn't need to. The way she looked at him during dinner was enough.

He still scrubbed his sneakers at night. Still taped the sole when it peeled. But now, when he walked the hallway, nobody pointed. Nobody chanted. They just made space— and sometimes, they nodded.

The notebook that carried him through the week filled fast. He retired it to the bottom of the stack and cracked open a new one, clean cover, pages waiting.

The first line he wrote:

Wars don't end when the crowd leaves. They end when the story changes.

And the story had changed.

Ridgeview still had cliques. Still had flash. Still had noise. But the scoreboard had been hacked. Kids wore what they wore, louder or quieter, with more choice in it now. Swagger wasn't just clothes. Swagger wasn't just crowns. Swagger was saying your name like it mattered. Swagger was stepping up when the room tried to shrink you. Swagger was claiming ground and letting the world catch up.

Jalen didn't become king. He didn't want to. He became something else. A marker. A reminder. A proof that sometimes, one voice—raw, shaky, steady—could tilt a hallway.

The next Showcase came a year later. Jalen was still there, notebook thicker, pace slower, voice deeper. Royalty performed too, slick as always. But this time, when Jalen walked up to the mic, no one whispered *boring*. No one laughed.

They leaned forward, ready for the truth.

Because Ridgeview had learned something the hard way:

Confidence doesn't come in labels.

It comes in voice.

And that lesson, like fire, spreads.

AUTHOR'S NOTE

When I started writing *Swagger Wars,* I kept asking myself one question: **what does it really mean to have swag?**

For a lot of young people, "swag" has been boiled down to labels—sneakers, phones, jewelry, and clothes. Social media shouts it louder, making it seem like what you wear decides your worth. But deep down, I think most of us know that's not the truth. The truth is harder, but better: swag is confidence. Swag is courage. Swag is showing up as yourself when it would be easier to hide.

Jalen's story is fiction, but it's built out of real hallways I've walked, real whispers I've heard, and real moments when kids were measured not by who they were, but by what they owned. Writing this book reminded me that the voices most people try to ignore—the quiet ones, the overlooked ones, the ones without the spotlight—are often the strongest.

If you've ever felt "out" because of your clothes, your shoes, or the things you couldn't afford, I wrote this for you. If you've ever been told you don't belong, I wrote this for you. If you've ever had to remind yourself that your worth can't be scanned like a bar-code, I wrote this for you.

Because the truth is, swagger can't be bought. It isn't rented or borrowed or stitched into a sleeve. It's lived. It's earned. It's carried in your bones, your words, and your name.

And when you decide to own that? The whole room will have no choice but to catch up.

So, wherever you are—school hallways, locker rooms, classrooms, or stages of your own—keep your ground. Speak your truth. Build your swagger from the inside out.

That's the real flex.

- **Joyce Lee**

RESOURCES & SUPPORT

Swagger is about more than style—it's about confidence, self-respect, and courage. If you've ever felt "out," know this: you are never alone, and your voice matters. Here are some resources that might help:

☎ **Hotlines & Support Services**

- **988 Suicide & Crisis Lifeline (U.S.)**
  Call or text 988 if you're in emotional distress or need someone to talk to right away.

- **Teen Line** – Call 310-855-4673 or text TEEN to 839863. A confidential hotline where trained teens listen and support.

Spirit, Inc. – helps with hygiene poverty in the Greater Houston area. www.spirit-np.info. Call 713-494-6063 or email spiritempowerment21@gmail.com

National Runaway Safeline – 1-800-RUNAWAY (1-800-786-2929). For youth in crisis or needing a safe plan.

🌍 **Online & Community Spaces**

- **DoSomething.org** – Youth-led campaigns about confidence, bullying, and social issues.

- **Poetry Out Loud (poetryoutloud.org)** – A spoken-word program that helps teens find their voice.

- **Boys & Girls Clubs of America** – After-school programs where leadership and confidence are built.

💡 Affirmations for Daily Swagger

- *My worth is not a price tag.*

- *I own my name. I own my ground.*

- *Labels don't define me—I define me.*

- *My voice is my loudest flex.*

✏️ Try This: The Notebook Challenge

Start your own "swagger notebook." Each day, write one line about who you are—not what you wear. By the end of a month, you'll have a book of proof that your confidence is growing from the inside out.

Swagger isn't about crowns, logos, or smoke machines. Swagger is standing up, saying your name, and believing you belong. Carry that truth with you—and never let anyone tell you different.